Evie and the Volunteers

Food Pantry

Book 4

By: Marcy Blesy

Cover design by Cormar Covers.

Follow my blog for information about upcoming books or short stories.

Chapter 1:

"Are you two about done?" asks Mom. "Dinner's ready in five minutes."

"Almost, Mom!" I yell from the living room. Dad is gluing a picture of Daisy onto my poster board. It sits in the middle of a heart I drew. I take a step back to admire our work. "It looks perfect, Dad," I say.

"I agree, Evie. If you don't get an *A*, you're switching schools." He laughs, loud and long. I love Dad's laughs.

"You're crazy, Dad. Good luck trying to convince Mom of *that!*"

"Uh, yeah, you're right. Anyway, no worries. Your project rocks."

I have to agree, but without Dad's help providing the gentle elbowing to keep me working, the poster board probably would have been pretty sloppy because I'd be rushed for time. Now it's not only done before dinner, but everything looks perfect. Our assignment was to create a display showing two things: one—things we are thankful for—and two—things we have done to help people. It's Thanksgiving in a few days. It seems like a good project assignment. Plus, with all the volunteering my friends and I have done this year, I have a lot of material I can share in my presentation when I show the poster board in class tomorrow. I can't help but stare at my dad as he picks up the paper trash left over from cutting out the pictures I used to decorate. It's so nice to have him home again— forever this time. At least, I hope it will be forever.

"You might freeze me if you keep staring, Evie," Dad says laughing.

"Sorry."

"Kind of weird having me back?" he asks, "even after a month?"

"I guess so," I say. I wish we could go back to cutting and gluing.

"I'm not going anywhere," he says.

"Uh-huh."

"Evie, look at me." He waits until our eyes meet. "I'm not going to leave again. I promise."

"Okay, Dad," I say. "I think dinner's ready." I lead the way into the kitchen and away from all this serious talk.

Chapter 2:

"Can you believe how over the top Celia was with her presentation?" I ask Logan and Franny as we sit down for lunch. I really wish Mom made my lunch today. Staring at the school's version of a walking taco makes me want to barf. No one should eat mustard-colored cheese—ever.

"Totally over-the-top," says Logan. "You'd think if you'd never known her that she was a saint or a queen or the President of the United States with all the *charitable work* she's done. Did anyone really believe that Beyoncé talked about this awesome kid who spends every waking moment helping others? Where's the evidence? *Prove it* is what I say."

"I think you guys are being a little harsh," says Franny.

We both turn and stare at our quiet friend, often the voice of reason. "Franny, *we* of all people know the value of volunteering and helping others, but Celia makes it sound like she spends every waking moment helping others—baking bread for the senior center, mowing lawns for her neighbors, organizing a card club to send mail to *every single person in the military?* Who writes cards? And who can organize that many people? I asked my dad and he never heard of Celia or her supposed military program."

"Maybe she just exaggerated a little bit," says Franny softly. "It's hard to compete with *Evie and the Volunteers.*"

"Or a lot bit," says Logan.

"And at least we don't brag," I say. "And speaking of volunteering, Grandma told me that the food pantry at church is opening next week, just in time for Thanksgiving. I think Dad and I have had enough time together after school. He's starting a new job soon, too. Anyone want to go to the church with me on Saturday to see what a food pantry is all about?"

"I have soccer in the morning," says Logan. "but get some information for me and maybe I can help another day."

"I can come," says Franny. "I'm meeting Becca at the library with her mom for a half hour around 10:00. Then I'm free."

"That's awesome," I say. "I'm glad you decided to stick with the after-school program. They're lucky to have you."

Franny blushes. "I'm lucky to have them. As soon as Becca chooses the books she wants read for the week, I'll ride my bike over to the church."

It's settled then. *Evie and the Volunteers* is reunited again at the food pantry. And who doesn't like food?

Chapter 3:

Mom and Dad went out for breakfast this morning. It's been their Saturday morning routine since Dad got home. I'm usually still asleep while they're gone anyway, so it doesn't bother me. But today I am up early to meet Grandma who is going to help out at the food pantry, too. Daisy is sleeping on the couch in the living room. She is banned from sleeping on the couch in the living room, which is why I can't stop laughing.

"Nice job, Daisy!" I lift her paw to give her a high-five. "What they don't know won't hurt them. I bet you'd keep my secrets, too, like the fact that I'm going to have a Twinkie for breakfast. I know you'll keep *that* secret."

Daisy lifts her head and yawns her approval. I'm so glad Daisy is home where she belongs. It didn't take her long at all to bond with me. I know she remembered that I was the one who tried to save her first. She and Dad are best buds, but sometimes she sneaks out of my parents' room and jumps on my bed. She's not supposed to be on beds, either, but I never tell. I guess Mom still has to prove her loyalty to Daisy because she's the only one in the family who doesn't get Daisy's full attention. Sometimes Daisy acts like Mom's not even in the room. Maybe she knows that Mom didn't want to adopt a dog while Dad was gone. I'm sure Daisy will come around eventually.

Grandma honks her horn from across the street at her house at exactly 9:30 a.m. I grab my bag, pet Daisy, and run out the door to meet her.

There are not very many cars outside the Shorewood Covenant Church on a Saturday morning. "What are we going to do today?" I ask Grandma, who is walking rather quickly for a woman of her age. I can barely keep up.

"Well, the church started collecting donations a month ago—non-perishable items. Today we organize them."

"What's a *non-perishable* item?" I ask, walking in step with Grandma now.

"It means food that won't spoil for a while, like canned goods or boxes of macaroni and cheese or rice or cake mixes—that sort of thing. It also means items like napkins, paper plates, hygiene supplies like soap, shampoo, etc."

"That makes sense," I say.

When we get to the church auditorium, I see the boxes of donations that Grandma described. It's a canned goods explosion. I'm not sure I've even seen this much toilet paper in a grocery store before.

A tall younger-looking man comes out of an office when he sees Grandma and me. "Helen, it's lovely to see you!" he says. "And this must be Evie. It's nice to finally put a face with the name." He sticks his hand out for me to shake. "I'm Pastor Perry."

"Like Katy Perry?" I ask because she is one of my favorite singers. "Or Perry the Platypus?" because Phineas and Ferb is my favorite cartoon.

He laughs. "No, just Perry Octobagues," but since that's more than a mouthful, I just go by Pastor Perry."

"That's awful! I don't blame you."

Grandma steps on my foot. I don't think I'm supposed to react the way I do, which is scream, but it hurt. Then Grandma gives me a look that tells me I'd better behave, and I am reminded to mind my manners.

"Sorry. I think Perry is a cool name."

"Thank you, Evie. So, there are already a few other ladies here to help, but we need as many people as we can get. As you can see, there is a lot of work to be done." He pans the room with his hands. "The pantry is going to be housed in the basement. We cleaned out two storage rooms that were holding about thirty years' worth of unused items. That's another story! We chose the basement because there is a private entrance there. It's our hope that the people that need our services can maintain their dignity and not feel ashamed for needing help. They can come and go in private without fear of being *outed* for coming to a food pantry. Of course, there is no shame in needing help, but tell that to the people that need it."

"Evie, I think I'll put your Grandma to work with her friends labeling the shelves in the basement. I will need you and your friends—when they get here—to be our heavy lifters, carrying the boxes to the basement. Did you bring your muscles today?" I flex my arms to show him that I did.

By the time I get the tenth box down to the basement (because I am counting boxes), Franny shows up. She walks in through the private entrance to the basement. I am super excited to see her. "Franny! Help! There's like forty more boxes of food and supplies upstairs that we need to bring downstairs. My arms are about to fall off!"

"Nice to see you, too, Evie," says Franny laughing.

Then she pushes her sleeves up her arm and follows me downstairs. Grandma and her friends Barbara and Julie are good at giving orders. "Over there! Canned vegetables on *that* table. No, that's shampoo, not lotion. Shampoo goes on the counter by the refrigerator." So many rules.

On our next trip down, I notice that Grandma and Barbara and Julie aren't alone. A boy about my age but a lot taller with blonde hair almost as long as my shoulder-length hair is standing next to a box of school supplies that didn't have a place yet when I brought it down earlier.

"Hi, Evie," he says waving.

I stop in my tracks even though the box of canned corn and green beans is about to rip my arm out of my socket. I don't like being recognized by someone that I swear I've never met before. "Uh, hi," I say. I guess I sound rude because Grandma is shooting me looks with her *eye* again.

Julie comes to my rescue. "Evie, this is my grandson Dax. The two of you used to play together when you were little. Don't you remember playing at the park in your neighborhood while your grandma and I would drink bad coffee from the park concession stand?"

She and Grandma share a laugh that is both evil and silly. There must be more to that story. I look more closely at Dax—such a strange name for a kid. Then I remember, and I wish I didn't. "Are you the kid that pulled off my doll's head and buried it in the sandbox?" I ask, still haunted by the memory of my beloved Annabel without her head.

Dax smiles. "Yeah, that was me. Still holding a grudge, I see." His smile is as evil as I remember it to be.

"Well, that was a long time ago," Grandma says. "Dax is here to help get this pantry up and running by Monday. Thanksgiving is Thursday. We have promised in our advertisements to open the week of Thanksgiving. The busier we are, the faster the work will be done. Evie, show Dax what to do."

"Gladly," I say. He follows me upstairs. I have never been so happy to see Franny before in my life. She is standing at the top of the stairs with a big box of paper towels. "Franny, this is Dax. Dax, this is Franny." I look at Dax. "Take that box downstairs and come back for more." Before Franny can say anything, I take the box from her hands and put it in Dax's hands, practically shoving him toward the first step. When he is gone, I pull Franny into Pastor Perry's office, which is empty.

"What's going on?" she asks. "Who is that guy? Why are you freaking out?"

"His name is Dax. He's Julie's grandson. We used to play together when we were little when our grandmas got together. He's a total jerk. Remember Annabel?"

"That weird doll you buried in a shoebox under your bed?"

"Yes!"

Her eyes get big. "*He's* the one who did that to Annabel?"

I shake my head *yes*.

"Well, this is going to be an interesting day."

Chapter 4:

Franny and I took a midday break to McDonald's which is a couple of blocks away from the church. I know that Grandma wanted me to take Dax, but no way was I going to do that. Plus, Logan lives near McDonald's, too. I wanted to go to her house and drag her back to the church with us.

When we got back to the church, *Evie and the Volunteers* was at full strength again. I must have looked confused because Pastor Perry came out of his office to talk to us. "Looking for something, Evie?" he asks smiling.

"Where are all of the boxes?" I ask.

"Isn't it amazing? Julie's grandson cleared the rest of the boxes out of here in no time."

"Uh, yeah, sure. That's great," I say, but I know Pastor Perry sees right through me. I wish I could tell him about Annabel, but something tells me I'd get a lecture about forgiveness that I don't want to hear right now. So, instead I grab Logan's hand and pull her toward the stairs to the basement. Franny follows with a little wave to the pastor.

"There you are, girls!" says Grandma. "Glad to see that you decided to come back."

"We were always coming back, Grandma. We were just hungry."

"While you were gone, Dax brought all of the boxes down. Wasn't that helpful?"

I think her eye is spasming the way it blinks a million times in Dax's direction. *What about all the boxes Franny and I brought down?* I want to say, but I don't. I fake it. "That was *so* kind of him." The whole time I am aware that Dax is standing in the corner of the room with a big grin on his face. I ignore him. "What can we do *now* to help?"

"Start organizing!"

Julie and Barbara point out the organization system in the basement food pantry. Canned vegetables sit next to the canned fruit. Boxed dinners fill a low shelf. Above them, rice has its own shelf. Cereal and oatmeal and granola bars and soups—everything has its place. Franny, Logan, and I are like a well-oiled machine, smooth like butter in the way we work as a team.

It's all going well until a box of Cap'n Crunch cereal goes flying off the shelves, sending little yellow nuggets of goodness all over the floor. Thankfully, the grandmas are upstairs talking to Pastor Perry. That saves me from having to hear a speech about being more responsible.

"Here, let me help with that," says Dax, bending down to start collecting the cereal.

"It's fine," I say. "My mistake, my mess." When I grab the Cap'n Crunch box out of his hands, maybe a little too forcefully, he goes tumbling backwards as he slips on the golden crunch, landing on his bottom, crunching everything underneath him.

Logan starts laughing. Franny giggles, too, politely hiding her smile behind her hands. I don't know whether to laugh or apologize because I know I embarrassed Dax. But when he starts laughing, a deep, belly laugh, I join in, too. Then the cereal starts flying, first one piece at a time. Then we're all grabbing handfuls in rapid fire pelleting attacks. Cap'n Crunch drips from my hair. Dax looks like he's wearing a polka-dot shirt the way the cereal clings to him. Logan tries catching clean pieces of cereal in her mouth that Franny throws to her from the box. Maybe volunteering at the food pantry, even with Dax, the boy who beheaded my beloved Annabel, won't be so bad after all.

That is my thought until I hear steps coming down the stairs toward the basement, and I know the rest of the day isn't going to be quite so fun.

Chapter 5:

I'm not used to spending a Saturday night alone in my bedroom, but that's where I've been banished for the night *after my little stunt at the church* as Mom repeated to me from Grandma's own words. She didn't believe me when I said that the cereal disaster was only a little accident sprinkled with a bit of fun. After all, we cleaned up the mess. The best part of the whole ordeal was learning that Dax isn't as big a jerk as I thought he'd be.

A pinging sound on the side of my bedroom wall catches my attention. It's a steady, soft pounding that continues at even times like a ping-pong ball hitting a….That's exactly what it sounds like. Someone is playing ping-pong against the side of my room. I pull the curtain away from my window and nearly fall over backwards as Dax's face greets me instead of a night full of stars.

"What are you doing here?" I say, but I know he can't hear me because my window is closed, so I open my window and repeat myself. "What are you doing here?"

"Geesh. I thought you'd never open that window. I'm a good ping-pong player, but I can't keep this up all night." He takes the ping-pong ball and bounces it from the cement sidewalk outside my window onto the paneling of our house and back.

"What do you want?" I ask. "And how did you know this was my room?"

"Well, seeing how angry your grandma was today at the church, and knowing what I know about parents, I kind of assumed you were grounded. This was the only room on this side of the house with a light on. I took my chances."

"And if you know so much about parents," I say, lowering my voice so that mine won't hear me, "how come you're not in trouble, too?"

"Oh, that's easy. I'm spending the weekend with my grandparents. That's the only reason I'm in town to begin with. Grandma Julie was mad, at first, but she's a pushover. Plus, I reminded her how many boxes of food I carried down the basement stairs—all by myself." He flexes his skinny arms for emphasis. It makes me laugh. "Plus, they think I'm sleeping upstairs in the guestroom. I told them I was all tuckered out from the big day. And before you ask, there is a nice body pillow under the covers of the guest bed so if Grandma comes to check on her sweet angel, she'll see *me* snoozing away!"

"Well, you have everything figured out, don't you? Something tells me you have snuck out of your house before."

"I will never confirm nor deny that thought." He smiles, showing off one dimple on the right side of his face. Odd to have only one dimple. "So, come on. Tell your parents you're going to bed and fluff up those pillows. We can't stay out *all* night."

"I'm not going anywhere with you!" I say, tightening the pony tail holder in my hair.

"Then don't come with me. Pretend I'm not even here, but I heard about a bonfire at the high school for homecoming, and everyone will know I don't belong if I don't go with a *local*." He says the word *local* like it's a dirty word.

"I'm in fifth grade!" I can't believe what Dax is saying. "Do you really expect a fifth grader to pass as a high school kid? They'll know we don't belong!"

"I'm in sixth grade." He straightens his shoulders to try and look more impressive. It doesn't work. "Just try— please! This town is so lame. I have to find something interesting to do. Plus, I bet they'll have s'mores. You can't pass up s'mores, can you?"

I sigh. I do have a weak stomach for chocolate and gooey marshmallows mixed together. "Wait by the garage. And I'm only going for an hour." I pull a hooded sweatshirt out of my closet. I cannot believe that I am doing this. I haven't done anything this bad since I snuck out of my grandparent's house with Logan to go to the beach. My community service punishment started because of that choice. Maybe this time it won't turn out so bad, either, though I sure better not get caught.

I go out into the hall to find my parents. They are in the kitchen playing cards which is kind of cute. "Dad, Mom, I'm tired. I'm going to go to bed," I say fake yawning.

"On a Saturday night?" Dad asks. He touches my forehead like he's checking my temperature.

"It was a big day at the food pantry today. Plus, since I've been sent to my room for the night, I can't find that many exciting things to do in there. I might as well sleep."

"Evie, don't do this," says Mom.

"Do what?" I ask.

"Don't act like we *overreacted* by sending you to your room tonight. You and your friends made a mess out of that food pantry. You know better than that."

"Sure, Mom. I get it. *Whatever.*"

"Get some sleep, honey. Tomorrow is another day, and Grandma is counting on your help again," says Dad, standing up to kiss the top of my head.

I really am glad he's home. "Goodnight, Daisy." I pat my dog on the top of her head before I go back to my room. She's sitting at Dad's feet, his ever-present companion. I am almost back to my room when I remember something important. "And there's no need to check on me. I'm really beat, and sometimes the light in the hallway wakes me up when you open the door." I hope they buy my story.

I stuff pillows under my blankets the way that Dax told me he did at his grandparent's house. I feel a little guilty. My parents would be so worried if they found me missing, but I'm bored sometimes, too.

Dax is standing under the maple tree by our garage. "It's about time you got here. I almost gave up hope."

"Give me a break. I'm not as good at being bad as you are," I say, punching him in the arm.

I take the skateboard that Dax hands to me. He rides his skateboard on the sidewalk in the direction of the high school which is a few blocks away. I follow him. As we get closer I can see the flames from the bonfire licking the sky. It is so cool. We stash the skateboards next to the school and try to blend in with the crowd of teenagers walking toward the bonfire which is behind the football field. There is a line of people at a table that must have the supplies for s'mores. That's where he heads.

"See, I told you this was a good idea," says Dax. "Nobody suspects a thing."

"I guess," I say.

We move closer to the table. A boy with purple hair throws his arm around the shoulders of the girl in front of us. She pushes his arm away and tells him to get lost. He looks like a sad puppy walking away. "You know, I was really mad at you for taking off Annabel's head," I say to Dax.

He looks at me as if he's confused. "Who is Annabel?"

"My doll! That was her name."

"You kind of need to get past that," he says. "Refresh my memory, though. I bet it's an amusing story."

I sigh. "When I was six, our grandmas took us to the park, the one in the middle of town with the metal circus animals."

"I remember that park. That giraffe was awesome."

"Yeah, it was. They took all the animals away last year because they were starting to wear out. I think they only needed to be restored. Anyway, I brought my favorite doll Annabel with me. You thought it would be a good idea to play hide-and-go-seek with Annabel. When you finally told me where Annabel was hiding after a *very* long time, I quit. But, you wouldn't give me Annabel. We fought over her. You grabbed her body, so when I pulled, her head popped off."

"Sounds to me like *you're* the one that pulled off Annabel's head."

I'm starting to remember why I don't like Dax after all. This night was a bad idea.

"Evie?"

The sound of my name snaps me back to attention. The fact that the sound of my name is being spoken by Mrs. Bender, my middle school counselor, and the director of the after-school program I just finished volunteering with—well, it terrifies me. "Uh, hello, Mrs. B. What are you doing here?" It's the first thing I can think to ask, but it's a stupid question. Mrs. Bender is married to *Mr. Bender*, the high school football coach. Plus, it's a small town and everyone always finds everything out. I am in so much trouble.

"She was hungry for a s'more," says Dax. "I'm Dax." He sticks his hand out and shakes Mrs. Bender's hand before she has time to ask me another question.

"It's nice to meet you, Dax." She smiles at him but not at me. He smiles back. "Evie, this homecoming event is for high school students. You can't be here."

"Sorry about that, Mrs. Bender," says Dax. "I'm new in town, and Evie wanted to show me around. We found this bonfire quite by accident." He flashes his pearly whites again.

"I didn't know there was a new student enrolling at M.W. Clinton Middle School. That *is* exciting news. I look forward to seeing you on Monday."

I feel my stomach start to churn. "Um, well, you see…"

Dax puts his hand on my shoulder. "I would *love* to attend school here. I'm staying with my grandparents this weekend while my parents look for houses in the county. I sure hope they pick this school district. Your bonfires are the bomb."

Before I look away, trying not to laugh with amusement or vomit with the thought of my getting busted by his lie, I see Dax wink at Mrs. B. He actually *winks* at her.

"Well, you two better get home now. It's getting late. I'm sure you can find a dessert at home. Shall I call your parents, Evie, and tell them that you will be home soon?"

"N…no, Mrs. B. Thanks. They said to be home by 9:30." I look down at the watch that I am not wearing under the sleeve of my sweatshirt. "Look at that. It's 9:15. We'd better go. Have fun. Tell Mr. Bender I said *good luck at the football game*." And we are out of the parking lot on our skateboards without another look back.

When we are back on the sidewalk that leads to my house, I stop to take what feels like my first breath. Dax stops, too.

He looks at me with a raised eyebrow and shakes his head. "*Good luck at the football game?*"

"What?" I ask super annoyed.

"Do you really think the high school football coach wants to hear a message like that from some lame middle school girl?"

"Don't be a jerk," I say. "I panicked!"

"You need to relax, Evie. I can talk us out of anything. We're home without any worries now, right?" he says, as we walk toward my driveway.

"Fine. You're right. No worries." But when we turn the corner and I see the garage lights blaring from our house and my dad sitting on the back of his pick-up truck, I know he's not star-gazing. He's looking for me. "I hope you get grounded for life," I say to Dax before accepting my fate, "because my life is about to end."

"Get inside this house right now, Evie," yells my dad, walking toward us. I have never seen him so mad. He's never yelled at me before. "And you, young man, get out of my sight before I tear you apart."

Who is this dad? I don't like him one bit.

Chapter 6:

Grandma is quiet as she drives toward the church. The silent treatment is worse than being yelled at by Mom and Dad last night.

How could you be so irresponsible, Evie? Didn't you learn your lesson the first time when you snuck out of your grandparent's house last summer? Didn't you learn anything about responsibility and respect during all of your hours volunteering? We are so disappointed. You can kiss any fun in your life good-bye. Give us your phone. We're locking your window. Forget about seeing Logan and Franny except at school. And that boy? Evie, you really messed up tonight.

On and on they'd gone for what seemed like hours. Dad's voice got louder and louder. I cried. And it wasn't even the *I'm going to pretend cry and make them feel so sorry for me that they'll go easy* kind of cry. No, they were real tears. Mostly, I was so mad that I'd let that stupid boy talk me into sneaking out of my house. And that dad was so disappointed in me.

This morning at 6:30 a.m., my mom switched on my bedroom light, knocking me out of a perfectly good dream about winning the lottery and buying my own private island away from all parents, to tell me to get up and get dressed because Grandma was coming to get me in fifteen minutes.

So, now I'm sitting next to Grandma on the quietest car ride I have ever taken. It's much too early to be up on a weekend, but Mom said that she had to let me go with Grandma because I'd committed to helping her at the food pantry. If I didn't fulfill my responsibilities it would be like punishing Grandma, not me. *Whatever.* I'm just glad to get away from my parents, especially my dad.

"We need to use our time wisely, Evie," says Grandma. The church is quiet as we pull into the parking lot. "Sunday school students and teachers won't arrive until 9:00. I want this pantry organized and clean. It's a reflection of our church outreach. Plus, we need to be ready for this week. The pantry opens tomorrow. With Thanksgiving on Thursday, it will be quite busy."

It's nice to hear Grandma's soft voice. "I'll work hard," I say.

She nods her head but says nothing more. In the basement of the church I work beside my Grandma, counting cans and boxes and bags, inventorying the supply so that the parishioners can be asked to donate any items that are lacking. It seems we are low on bathroom items like soap and shampoo. It is hard to understand how someone could have a hard time getting enough money to buy something so simple like soap. The people I know sure don't seem like they'd need to use a food pantry. Truth be told, when I heard about the church wanting to start a food pantry, I didn't even think there'd be a use for one. I still have my doubts.

I spy a few pieces of Cap'n Crunch cereal on the shelves in between cans of fruit—peaches, pears, and pineapple. I quietly pick them up and throw them away. Yesterday was so fun and so miserable. I hate days that end up letting you down when they start with such promise.

"Looks like we are almost set, Evie," says Grandma. "I need to take this list of needed items upstairs to Pastor Perry before church starts."

"Okay," I say. "I'll wait here."

"I think you should come with me. It will be nice having company in church today. Grandpa's been out of sorts lately with this colder weather. I've been keeping him at home."

I know better than to argue with her. "Sure, Grandma," I say, running my hands along the boxes of macaroni and cheese.

Grandma starts toward the stairs but stops and turns back toward me. I have to stop myself from running into her. "I know your dad was really angry last night, Evie," she says. "Your mom called me after you went to bed."

"Mad is an understatement," I say. "It was more like furious with a dose of crazy thrown in."

"Your dad has some difficulty processing things."

"What do you mean?" I ask.

"It means that he has trouble sometimes handling stress. He has to remind himself that the stresses he has at home are different than the stresses he had when he was fighting in the war. He gets that confused sometimes. But—he loves you. Never forget that."

I don't tell Grandma that last night was the first time I wished Dad would go back to his old apartment across the state. He was more fun when he visited us on the weekends.

Chapter 7:

I spend the rest of the weekend in my room. It's where I've been sent to live out my one month grounding when I don't have somewhere I have to be. I started reading a new book. I forgot how easy it is to escape into the world of a good book. My book is set during the future where everything seems too good to be true. I know that something bad is going to happen soon, but for now I like the perfect world I am reading about.

My friends attack me with hugs on Monday morning at school. It feels good to be reminded that I am still loved.

"Evie! You poor *thing!*" says Logan.

"How are you holding up?" asks Franny.

"Well, it stinks to be grounded," I say.

"I bet it does. It's all that stupid boy's fault," says Logan. "If he'd not visited his grandma this weekend, you never would have snuck out of your house!" She puts her hands on her hips as if she can't believe that Dax would do such a thing. It reminds me of Tipper's spunky attitude which makes me smile.

"You're right about that," I say. Franny looks like she has something to say but doesn't. "What is it, Franny?" I ask. "Just say whatever is on the tip of your tongue."

"No, you've been through too much."

"Say it!"

Mrs. Bender saves her as she walks toward us in the hall, but I already know what she wants to say. She's the practical one of the group after all. She wants to tell me that even though it was Dax's idea to sneak out, it was my decision to actually do it. I hate to admit when the people I care about are right.

"Hello, girls," says Mrs. Bender. "Can I see you for a minute, Evie?" she asks. It's hard to say *no* when she smiles so sweetly.

I look back at my friends. "Save me a seat in English," I say.

In Mrs. Bender's office, I pick up the mad-faced toad. Mrs. Bender notices but doesn't comment on my choice. "Evie, your Mom and I talked this morning on the phone."

"My Mom?"

"Yes. She asked me to speak with you. She told me that you didn't exactly have permission to go to the bonfire." She pauses for me to confirm this truth, but I don't say anything. "She told me how you snuck out of the house and how angry your parents were with you." She pauses again but gets nothing from me. "She wants to know how you're feeling about that, but she knows you might not want to talk to her right now."

"Nope and, no offense, but I don't want to talk to you, either."

I toss mean-faced toad onto her desk and run out of Mrs. Bender's office, nearly knocking Celia over. I wonder why she looks like she's one second away from bursting into tears. She has no idea how unfair life can be. Her life's so perfect.

After school, I stop at Grandma and Grandpa's house to see how the first day of the food pantry went. Grandpa is resting in his recliner with his feet up. Grandma has tucked a blanket around his feet.

"Hi, Grandma," I say, sinking into a chair at the kitchen table. I don't understand how she knows when company is coming over, but she dishes up a warm bowl of blueberry crisp the minute I sit down. It's delicious.

"Is everything okay, Evie?" she asks, as I lick the remainder of sweet splendor from the bottom of the bowl.

"Oh, sorry. No, nothing's the matter. I just wondered how the food pantry went today. You know—was it busy?"

"Unfortunately, it was much busier than we anticipated it would be. There are many items we are running short of already."

"Really? Like what?" I ask.

"Several church members donated fresh fruits and vegetables, milk, bread—things that don't have a long shelf life before they expire. They are nearly gone. We need to find a way to stock fresh items. Nobody deserves to live on boxed and canned goods." Grandma sighs. She has such a big heart.

Grandpa's television blares from the front room. I listen to the commercials. A lightbulb goes off in my brain.

I jump up from the table and nearly knock my chair over. "I think I can help," I say.

"Where are you going, Evie?" she asks.

"Oh, drat! I'm grounded. Grandma, can you do me a *huge* favor?"

"What is it, Evie?"

"Can you drive me somewhere so Mom and Dad don't think I'm ignoring their rules? I would ride my bike, but that wouldn't go over so well."

"Evie, are you sure you have to go somewhere today? I don't want to upset your parents, and Grandpa needs me to be here in case there's a problem."

"What kind of problem?" I ask.

"He's just not feeling like himself," she says.

"Oh, okay. I think I better go home then. Thanks for the blueberry crisp." I kiss Grandpa on the cheek on my way out the door. He kind of moans in his sleep. It makes me sad. "I'll go to the pantry with you on Wednesday—if Mom and Dad let me. We don't have school because of Thanksgiving vacation," I yell to Grandma as I close the door.

When I get home, I do a Google search for the phone number of the local grocery store, the one that played their ad from Grandpa's television. They have a home-bound delivery program for people that can't do their own grocery shopping. I was reminded of that commercial when Grandpa's television was blaring while I ate my blueberry crisp. I remember watching the commercial when I used to be allowed to watch television before my grounding.

I punch in the number to Friendly Foods. "Hello, my name is Evie. Can I speak with a manager, please?"

I explain that I am a volunteer at the Shorewood Covenant Church's new food pantry and that they are running short of non-perishable items. Since it's Thanksgiving week, I tell them that I need them to bring over some of their best loaves of fresh bread, some bags of potatoes, broccoli, and lettuce. I also ask for eggs and milk. The manager asks me, at first, if this is some kind of joke because they don't usually make delivery for kids. I promise that I am telling the truth and even mention my Grandma's name. Everyone knows Grandma in town. Then I tell him I have money in my piggy bank that I didn't spend from my birthday and last year's Christmas plus money my grandparents sometimes give me for good report cards. Then he promises to have a delivery man at our house in a half hour. I check the time. That will be cutting it close. My parents will be home within the hour. I'm afraid they will turn the delivery man away. I shut off my phone and hope for the best.

At 5:15, fifteen minutes before my parents might arrive, I see the delivery truck from Friendly Foods pull into our driveway. I meet the man in the driveway before he can ring the doorbell. He seems surprised. "Hello," I say. "I'm Evie. Thanks for getting here so fast, but I really need you to get out of here before my parents get home."

The driver smiles. "I remember that feeling." I hand him two twenty dollar bills, plus a five and seven singles. "Is this enough?" I ask.

"Happy Thanksgiving, Evie—compliments of the boss." He nods at the groceries in the back of his truck.

"I don't understand."

"Mr. Davis told me to tell you these groceries are on the house."

"On the house?" I ask confused.

"It means that they are free—compliments of Friendly Foods. You impressed him with your desire to help others. Plus, he told me to give you his card." He pulls a card from his pocket and hands it to me. "Mr. Davis wants your food pantry director to call him after the holidays. He'd like to talk about setting up a more steady donation plan—a way of donating food the grocery store would have to throw out—but nothing spoiled or bad."

I can't believe what I am hearing. This is too good to be true. And I only wanted to make things right for Thanksgiving.

"You'd better take these items. Some of them need to be refrigerated."

He hands me two bags full of loaves of bread. Then he places other bags full of fresh vegetables and fruit onto the sidewalk leading up to my house. Before he leaves, he reaches into his car and pulls out a box that holds four pumpkin pies. I feel like crying. "Thank you." That's all I can get out without turning into a blubbering kid.

"Do you need help getting those things into your house?"

"No, thanks. We have an extra refrigerator in our garage. Tell Mr. Davis that I really appreciate his generosity."

I am putting the last items into the refrigerator when the garage door opens. It's my dad's pick-up truck. At first I think Dad is going to be mad at me because I'm not in the house doing my homework. Instead, the first thing he does when he gets out of his truck is hold out his arms asking for a silent hug. And I fall into his arms like it's the safest place in the world. We stand there in the garage—me crying into his chest and him crying into the top of my head. I can only imagine what Mom is thinking when she pulls her car into the garage next. She gets out of the car and joins us for a family hug. It's the best feeling in the world.

Chapter 8:

I'm still grounded, but things have thawed a bit at home. I still can't watch television or have my phone or hang out with Logan or Franny, but I don't have to hide in my room, either. My parents were kind of surprised by all the food in the garage refrigerator, too. When I explained how I got it, though, they seemed happy. Mom even shed a tear. She took the food to the church this morning on her way to work and promised to pass Mr. Davis' card to Pastor Perry. Tomorrow I'm going to the church with Grandma to work in the food pantry. We get to start our Thanksgiving vacation a day early from school.

Dad just beat me in a game of Battleship. I am putting the pieces away, pulling the red and white pegs from the boards. The doorbell rings. Mom answers the door. I can hear her talking, but I don't know what she's saying.

"Evie, there is someone here to see you," she says.

My dad follows me into the living room. I hear him whisper *what's he doing here?* under his breath. Then Mom puts her hand on his back and leads him toward the kitchen. I am left alone with Dax—the last person I want to see.

I repeat my dad's question. "What are you doing here?"

He shuffles from foot to foot, staring at the tile on our floor. I can see a car parked in the driveway. It looks like his Grandma Julie's car. "I—I am sorry I got you in trouble."

"Okay," I say.

"That's it?" he asks.

"What do you want me to say?"

"That maybe you don't blame me for getting you into trouble because you actually had fun and wanted to come with me—something like that, maybe?"

"I don't blame you, Dax. I wish you'd never come to spend the week with your grandparents because I wouldn't have snuck out to the bonfire on my own, but I didn't have to go with you if I didn't want to. It was stupid but kind of fun at the same time—before I got caught."

Dax laughs. "I have way too much fun making stupid decisions."

"Maybe it would have been good to know this information about you sooner."

"Well, anyway, I have something I wanted to give you before I leave." He reaches into a bag he's holding and pulls out a box. He hands it to me.

"What is it?" I ask.

"Look for yourself."

I pull the lid off the shoebox. I can't believe what I see. The box slips out of my hand but not before I pull out the beautiful doll inside. "Annabel?" I ask. "How did you…?"

"It's not really your doll—the one that you had before. But, yesterday Grandma Julie and I went to a thrift store. They had that stupid doll there." He points to Annabel's twin. "I thought you might like to have it, since the head is still attached and all." He smiles again.

"Thanks, Dax."

He smiles shyly. "Yeah, you're welcome. You'd better get her out of my view, though, or I can't promise what will happen to her."

"You don't have to be a jerk forever, you know?" I say.

"I guess I don't. But sometimes it's more fun."

I play push him toward the door. "Get out of here."

"Gladly." I watch him walk out the door and down the sidewalk toward his grandma's car. "See you around, Evie," he says.

I wave *goodbye* and carry my new Annabel back into the house. Boys are so weird.

Chapter 9:

I help Grandma load a donation of laundry detergent into the back of her car. Women from her Monday night card group took up a collection to buy laundry supplies for the food pantry. People really do have kind hearts. It doesn't always seem that way. I think it's because people don't always know what they need to do to help. Sometimes telling someone exactly what to do makes it easier for everyone.

"I need to check on Grandpa before we leave," she says, wiping sweat off her forehead.

"It's okay, Grandma. I'll check on him. You start the car." She smiles and nods her head.

I let myself into the house, closing the back door quietly. Grandpa loves to tell me that he's sick and tired of me slamming that door. It's only taken me a few years to remember. He is resting in his recliner again, his legs propped up higher than the rest of his body.

"Hi, Grandpa. We're leaving for the food pantry. Is there anything you need?"

"Meredith?"

I wrinkle my forehead until my head hurts. "Huh?"

"Meredith, get me another blanket."

"Grandpa, it's not Meredith. It's Evie. *I'm Evie.* Meredith is in college. But she's coming home tomorrow for Thanksgiving. Remember?"

"Oh. Sure. Evie, get me a blanket.'"

I take one of Grandma's famous homemade afghans, a fancy word for a blanket I think, and tuck it in around Grandpa. Then I find the remote control and set it next to the arm of his chair. "Do you want me to change the channel while I'm here?"

"No. Leave it. The noon news is coming on soon."

I look at the clock. It's only 9:30a.m. "Okay, Grandpa. Grandma and I are leaving now. She will be home in a few hours. Call her cell phone if you need something." I point to the house phone on his side table.

"Okay. Okay. Get going now. You're blocking the television."

Something doesn't seem right about leaving him alone, but I don't mention it to Grandma. She's one ball of knotted up stress this morning, like her yarn looks after Mr. Stinkypants finds it. At least the cat will keep Grandpa company.

The food pantry is busy when Grandma and I arrive. Barbara and Julie are helping people load their bags with items for their families. Dax is nowhere to be found. Thank goodness.

"Good morning, Evie." It's Pastor Perry. His hands are full with a box of assorted canned goods. "Glad you could help out. We have a lot of last minute families stopping in for the holiday tomorrow. Can you please get the door?"

I hold the door open. He follows a woman to her car. She is young and carries a toddler on her hip. As I'm watching the woman settle her baby into the car, a van pulls into the parking lot. I can tell there are a lot of people inside because I can already hear them, even with the windows up. I let the pantry door close shut so they don't see me staring. It slams kind of loud, though, just like Grandma's back door. She looks up from next to the cereal shelf she is reorganizing. She doesn't look happy. I mouth *I'm sorry* as the door opens again, slamming shut *again* after the van family piles inside the cramped food pantry. A mom, dad, and a set of rowdy boys that remind me of Chase and Chance start pulling items of food from the shelves. The mom keeps smacking the hands of the little boys who aren't taking the things that the family needs.

"Can I help you?" Grandma asks the mom and dad while Julie tries to distract the boys.

"Yes, please," says the mom quietly. She hands a list to Grandma. "I'm sorry. My daughter is supposed to be coming in to watch her brothers. She's being a bit difficult today." Just then the door opens. "There she is," says the mom to Grandma. "Celia, take your brothers outside. They are not helping."

Celia? That's not a common name at all. I can't believe it. It's Celia from school—Celia who tells everyone how perfect she is and how perfect her life is. What is she doing here? I don't mean to make a scene. The last thing I want is for Celia to know that I've seen her at a food pantry, but when I take a step back toward the church stairs, my hand brushes the counter and a can of tuna salad crashes to the floor. It makes a loud noise and rolls right in the direction of Celia. Grandma shakes her head at me disapprovingly again. Celia's eyes freeze when they meet my own.

"Celia, I told you to take your brothers outside. Your dad and I will be there soon. Please."

"My granddaughter can help, too, if you'd like," says Grandma. "She's helping me this morning."

I know Grandma means well, but she doesn't understand. She doesn't know. She doesn't know Celia. She doesn't know that my knowing that Celia doesn't live the perfect *I have everything life* that she wants people to think she lives is a big deal.

"I'll take them," she says. Celia grabs a hand from each of her brothers and pulls them out the door, slamming the door shut louder than ever before.

"We really need to fix that door," laughs Pastor Perry as he comes back inside. "So, who needs help?" If only his smile could solve all the problems in the world.

Chapter 10:

"Holiday, pass the potatoes!" says my sister Meredith to me.

She's the only one who calls me that. My name makes her think of Christmas Eve, so she calls me *Holiday*.

"Earth to Holiday. What's wrong with you?" she says.

"Sorry." I pass the mashed potatoes, piping hot with lots of melted butter on top. Grandma's table always looks so pretty at family dinners with her dainty lace tablecloth. It's extra special today with her Pilgrim salt and pepper shakers.

"She's been a busy girl volunteering all over town. My friend Julie even asked her to volunteer at the public library this winter," says Grandma beaming.

"I hear she's had a little time exploring the high school, too," says Meredith. "Ouch! Who kicked me under the table?"

Mom gives Meredith the *evil eye*. I'm glad I'm not the only one who gets that look. "That will be enough," says Mom.

"Tell us more about your internship," says Dad to Meredith.

I don't really listen to Meredith talk. I feel like I'm in a bubble, my little family complete again with plenty of food to eat, a nice place to live, and extras of anything I need available. Daisy rubs up against my leg, another blessing this year. I can't believe that Grandma let us bring her over for the day. Mr. Stinkypants has been hiding ever since Daisy bounded in the front door. Then I think about those people from the food pantry like Celia. Why do they have so much less? Grandma says that people who need

67

help don't always need it forever—that sometimes life knocks you out for a few rounds before you bounce back. I think it's just not fair.

"Grandpa!" Meredith screams as she jumps up from the table, snapping me back to Thanksgiving dinner.

"Call 911, Bill," says Mom to Dad.

Dad jumps up and pulls his phone from his pocket while I watch Meredith and Mom lower Grandpa to the floor from his slumped over position at the table. He has cranberry sauce stuck to his chin. I want to wipe his face, but I'm too scared to move. Grandpa looks like he's having trouble breathing. He isn't talking.

"Open the front door and flag the paramedics in when the ambulance arrives," says Dad to me. He is following the 911 operator's orders and checking for Grandpa's pulse.

I do as Dad says. Within minutes, the paramedics are here working on Grandpa. They find a pulse and put an oxygen mask on his face. Grandma is holding his hand and stroking his hair. He still has cranberry sauce on his chin. They put him on a stretcher with wheels and roll him into the ambulance. Mom grabs her jacket, and she and Dad and Grandma pile into Grandma's car to go to the hospital. Dad sits in the driver's seat. He is very calm, not panicking at all. Then they are gone.

"It's going to be okay, Holiday," says Meredith. She puts her arms around me. I cry on her shoulder while Daisy squeezes in between our legs, aware that things are definitely not right with our little family. I want to go back into our safe bubble. Instead I get into Meredith's car, and we drive to the hospital.

At the hospital, Mom gives me money to buy a candy bar at the vending machine in the cafeteria. It's not exactly a turkey dinner. The cafeteria is full. There are three long tables set up where people are serving food. A sign above the table says *Free Thanksgiving Meal.* Guests are taking their trays down the tables and getting piles of yummy Thanksgiving food piled onto their plates. I guess if your loved one has to spend the holiday in the hospital, it's nice to still get a good meal that feels home-cooked. Mom says we can finish dinner at home.

I sit down at a table in the far corner of the cafeteria to eat my candy bar. Grandpa has been admitted to a room. He's talking again, which is good.

"Are you stalking me?" asks someone standing in front of me.

I follow the shoes up to her face. I can't believe I am looking at Celia. "I'm not stalking you, Celia. This is the last place I want to be. My Grandpa's been admitted. The doctors think he had a heart attack."

"Oh. Sorry," she says. She kicks at nothing in particular on the floor.

"Why are you here?"

"My little brother cut his foot on a nail. They said he doesn't need stitches."

"That's good," I say.

"You know, my parents just stopped at the food pantry yesterday because they saw a sign outside the church about pumpkin pies. They thought it would help the church if they bought some pies."

"Sure, Celia," I say. "That's fine."

"It's true! And don't tell anyone. We wouldn't want every church in town knowing we were willing to donate our money. We don't have time to save everyone, you know?" She shrugs her shoulders.

I throw away my candy bar wrapper and head back toward the elevators that will take me to Grandpa's room.

Then I remember that I left my change from the candy bar machine sitting on the table. When I walk back into the cafeteria Celia and all of her family, her parents and her brothers, are in line with their trays to receive the Thanksgiving meal for patient's families. I know that Celia's brother isn't a patient. I wonder if his injury is even real. I guess Celia's family needed a warm meal today. It's Thanksgiving, after all. I'll never tell Celia's secret. Even though she lies to protect that family secret, she wasn't lying about one thing—her family is perfect in one way— they perfectly love each other. You don't need money for that.

Chapter 11:

Grandpa has been home for a couple of days. He's back to himself, barking orders at everyone. Grandma loves it. And Grandpa loves Grandma. I know he does. He's having surgery on his heart next week. There is a blockage where his blood doesn't flow right. That's why he was a little forgetful and had trouble breathing. The body needs the blood to flow correctly in order for everything to work right. Heart surgery is scary, but I know he's going to be fine.

"I think your grounding is over now," says Dad. We are sitting on the front porch, soaking in the rays from an unusually warm late November day.

"I thought you and Mom said I was grounded until the end of the year," I say, petting Daisy with my fuzzy socks.

"Mr. Davis called today."

"What did he want?"

"He told me that he's finalized the details with Pastor Perry about how the grocery store is going to donate non-perishable items to the food pantry. Sometimes they have surplus or items about to expire but still perfectly safe—things like that."

"That's great," I say.

"It is pretty great," says Dad. "And you did that, Evie."

"It was just an idea for Thanksgiving food at first," I say.

"It was a good idea," says Dad. "You goof up sometimes, Evie. But you have a good heart." He ruffles my hair.

"Just like you, Dad?" I ask. I don't mean to be sassy.

Dad pauses before speaking. I think he's going to yell at me again. "Just like me," he says. Then he laughs— long and loud and hard. And I laugh, too.

Maybe being imperfect is the perfect way to live my life if I have other imperfect people to love me through it.

Evie and the Volunteers Series

Join ten-year-old Evie and her friends as they volunteer all over town meeting lots of cool people and getting into just a little bit of trouble. There is no place left untouched by their presence, and what they get from the people they meet is greater than any amount of money.

Book 1   Animal Shelter

Book 2   Nursing Home

Book 3   After-School Program

Book 4   Food Pantry

Book 5: Coming March 2017

Other Children's Books by Marcy Blesy:

Confessions of a Corn Kid:

Twelve-year-old Bernie Taylor doesn't fit in. She wants to be an actress but not your typical country-music lovin', beef-eatin' actress you'd expect from Cornville, Illinois. No way. She wants to go to Chicago to be a real actress, just like her mom did before she died of breast cancer. Bernie keeps a journal that her Mom gave her and writes down all her confessions, the deepest feelings of her heart, 'cause she doesn't want any of those regrets Mom talked about. Regrets sound too much like those bubbly blisters she keeps getting on her feet from trying to fit into last year's designer knock-off shoes. But it's not easy for Bernie to pursue her dreams. Her dad just doesn't understand. Plus, she's tired of being bullied for being different. Why can't middle schoolers wear runway fashions to school?

Then, during the announcement of the sixth grade play, Bernie's teacher reveals that there will be one scholarship to a prestigious performing arts camp in Chicago. Bernie knows it's her one big chance to achieve her dream. She spends too much time dreaming of the lead role in the play (which includes kissing Cameron Edmunds) and not enough time practicing her audition lines. She bumbles her lines, blows her audition, and battles her bully, Dixie Moxley, reigning Jr. Miss Corn Harvest Queen. She digs in with the heels of her hand-me-down knee-high boots, determined to win that scholarship-somehow. If she doesn't, she'll be stuck in Cornville forever, far away from the spotlight she craves.

Am I Like My Daddy? :

Join seven-year-old Grace on her journey through coping with the loss of her father while learning about the different ways that people grieve the loss of a loved one. In the process of learning about who her father was through the eyes of others, she learns about who she is today because of her father's personality and love. *Am I Like My Daddy?* is a book designed to help children who are coping with the loss of a loved one. Children are encouraged to express through journaling what may be so difficult to express through everyday conversation. *Am I Like My Daddy?* teaches about loss through reflection.

Am I Like My Daddy? is an important book in the children's grief genre. Many books in this genre deal with the time immediately after a loved one dies. This book focuses on years after the death, when a maturing child is reprocessing his or her grief. New questions arise in the child's need to fill in those memory gaps.

Be the Vet:

Do you like dogs and cats?

Have you ever thought about being a veterinarian?

Place yourself as the narrator in seven unique stories about dogs and cats. When a medical emergency or illness impacts the pet, you will have the opportunity to diagnose the problem and suggest treatment. Following each story is the treatment plan offered by Dr. Ed Blesy, a 16 year practicing veterinarian. You will learn veterinary terms and diagnoses while being entertained with fun, interesting stories.

This is the first book in the BE THE VET series.

For ages 9-12

40164838R00052

Made in the USA
Middletown, DE
05 February 2017